DATE DUE

MAY 1 4 2003	MAR 0 2 2005	
AUG 1 8 2003	MY 06 05	
SEP 0 3 2003	NOV 2 0 2006	
SEP 2 3 2003		
NOV 0 7 2003	MAR 1 3 2007	
MAR 2 3 2004	MAY 2 9 2007	
APR 2 8 2004		OCT 0 8 2007
MY Jul 1 4 2004		
SEP 0 1 2004	MAR 0 8 2010	
NOV 0 8 2004	FE 23 '11	
JAN 2 5 2005		

George Shannon

Lizard's Guest

Pictures by Jose Aruego
and Ariane Dewey

Greenwillow Books
An Imprint of HarperCollinsPublishers

Lizard's Guest
Text copyright © 2003 by George W. B. Shannon
Illustrations copyright © 2003 by Jose Aruego and Ariane Dewey
All rights reserved. Manufactured in China.
www.harperchildrens.com

Pen and ink, gouache, and pastels were
used to prepare the full-color art.
The text type is Comic Sans.
The display type is Fontesque.

Library of Congress Cataloging-in-Publication Data
Shannon, George.
Lizard's guest / George Shannon ;
illustrated by Jose Aruego and Ariane Dewey.
p. cm.
"Greenwillow Books."
Summary: While dancing around, Lizard accidentally steps on Skunk's toes
and then promises to take care of lazy Skunk until his foot is healed.
ISBN 0-06-009083-9 (trade). ISBN 0-06-009084-7 (lib. bdg.)
[1. Lizards—Fiction. 2. Skunks—Fiction. 3. Honesty—Fiction. 4. Laziness—Fiction.]
I. Aruego, Jose, ill. II. Dewey, Ariane, ill. III. Title.
PZ7.S5287 Lf 2003   [E]—dc21   2002023548

First Edition 10 9 8 7 6 5 4 3 2 1

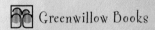 Greenwillow Books

For Barbara H. Berger
&
Kathryn O. Galbraith
—C.S.

For Juan
—J. A. & A. D.

Lizard danced with his shadow in the rising sun.

"Sing zing-a-ling.
Sing a zoli-o.
Follow me
And around we'll go!"

He danced with a skip.

Two backward hops.

Spun around with a jump and—

"Ouuuuuuch!" screamed Skunk.
"You STOMPED my toes."
"Oh! I'm sorry," said Lizard. "Will you be all right?"
"Do I *look* all right?" Skunk winced.
"I'll have to crawl back home."

"No, you won't," Lizard said.
"Let me help you to my rock. I'll take care of you
 till you're as good as new."
 Skunk grinned. "Promise?"
"Promise," said Lizard. "Whatever it takes."

"Cool mud for my toes and some water would be nice," said Skunk. "*And* a snack. I've got to eat well so my toes can heal."
"Coming up," said Lizard.

Skunk watched till Lizard was out of sight.

Then he stood and stretched.

He was playing hopscotch when Lizard came back.

"You're healed!" Lizard cried.

Skunk collapsed on the rock. "I *tried*.
But they're just too sore!"

"But you looked so strong," said Lizard.
"Let me help you try again."

Skunk's tail stood up and began to twitch.
"Then again," said Lizard, "it's never ever good
to try to walk too soon!"

"Never ever," Skunk agreed. "Crunchy bugs
and a nap are all I need right now.
And perhaps some leaves to make a small fan."

When Lizard came back, Skunk was dancing on his rock.

But when Skunk saw *Lizard*, Skunk collapsed on the rock
with his sore-toe-poor-me face again.
"Every time I try," Skunk said, "it just gets worse."
"Maybe later?" asked Lizard.

Skunk's tail went up and began to twitch.
"Or tomorrow?" Lizard said. "Or the day after that?"

Lizard didn't *dare* risk ever making Skunk mad.
He couldn't sing or nap on a rock that stunk of skunk.
"Is there anything you need?" Lizard asked.

"Some grubs and tender sprouts would really hit the spot. And a canopy of flowers would be *so* nice. It's impossible to rest in the blinding sun." Skunk grinned. "Whatever it takes, just as you said. And it *could* take days."

Lizard slowly nodded. "Oh, yes. I *see*."
As Lizard left, Skunk called, "And don't be so skimpy. You never bring enough!"

Lizard came back with grubs and flowers and tender sprouts.
He quickly made a canopy. And propped Skunk's foot on a
mound of sand.

Lizard hurried back and forth all morning long,
bringing Skunk all he wanted and a little bit more.

"Dear me!" said Lizard. "You look a little worse.
Is there anything else you think might help?"
"A story or a song might help me rest," said Skunk.
"Of course," Lizard said. "A promise is a promise.
Whatever it takes. But first I'll get fresh flowers
for the canopy."

Lizard sang with a smile as he left again.

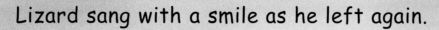

"Sing zing-a-ling.

Sing a zoli-o.

Follow me

And around we'll go!"

Skunk waited and watched as the sun crossed the sky.
From time to time he heard a "zoli-o" in the distance,
but it never came near.
"Li . . . zard!" called Skunk. "Liiiiiii . . . ZARD!"

When the sun began to set, Skunk climbed on the rock.
"You can't count on a lizard doing anything right."
Skunk looked all around. "L . . . I . . . Z . . . A . . . R . . . D!"
Not a sight. Not a sound.

Skunk limped a little way. "Lizard? I need fresh bugs."
"LIZARD! And some cool, fresh mud. Li...zard?
You said you'd sing me a song."

When limping took too long, he began to walk, then finally to run.

"LIZARD! I need more grubs.

L . . . I . . . Z . . . A . . . R . . . D!"

Skunk called and called till his voice gave out.
In the quiet he heard a distant "zoli-o."
Skunk ran toward the song as Lizard's voice grew.

"Lizard!" shouted Skunk.
"You're healed!" Lizard cried.

Skunk's tail went up and began to twitch.
"Was this a trick?" asked Skunk.
Lizard smiled with a shrug.
"A promise is a promise. Whatever it takes.
But whatever it *was*, it's a party now!"
"For who?" demanded Skunk.

"A party for us!
To celebrate *you* feeling fine again."

"Oh?" Skunk's tail went down. Then it began to sway as they sang "zoli-o" and danced through the evening in the fragrant breeze.